WALT DISNEY WORLD® RESORT

100 YEARS
OF
MAGIC

Disney
EDITIONS

For Disney Editions
Editorial Director: Wendy Lefkon
Assistant Editor and Additional Text: Jody Revenson

For Roundtable Press, Inc.
Directors: Susan E. Meyer, Marsha Melnick, Julie Merberg
Editor: John Glenn
Design Concept: Richard Berenson, Berenson Design Ltd.
Text: Pam Brandon
Project Coordinator, Computer Production, Photo Editor, Designer: Steven Rosen

ISBN 0-7868-5358-1

First Edition
2 4 6 8 10 9 7 5 3 1

TABLE OF CONTENTS

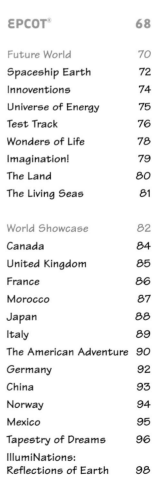

EPCOT®

INTRODUCTION

Once upon a time, a small-town boy, inspired by the tales of romance and adventure he read by the glow of a lantern's light, dreamed of bringing his own gift for story-telling and his fascination with technological innovation to the world.

Walt Disney's boundless enthusiasm, inspiring ingenuity, and creative energy are reflected in every facet of the Walt Disney World Resort. As Walt's brother Roy stated at the dedication in 1971, "Walt Disney World is a tribute to the philosophy and life of Walter Elias Disney...and to the talents, the dedication, and the loyalty of the entire Disney organization that made Walt Disney's dream come true."

This year, Walt Disney World Resort marks the 100th anniversary of the birth of Walt Disney with a spectacular celebration in honor of the dreams he brought to life. From the beloved characters who stroll the evocative, timeless paths of Magic Kingdom Park, and the international showplace and ever-evolving imaginative attractions of Epcot®, to the adventures of nature and exploration in Disney's Animal Kingdom Theme Park, and the high-energy excitement of the Disney-MGM Studios, Walt Disney's legacy is an extraordinary gift of magical creativity and dreams that will continue to enlighten and inspire all those who share it for many years to come.

The Magic Kingdom is a vacation classic, a place of timeless enchantment where the dreams of Walt Disney live on. In seven happy lands of yesterday, tomorrow, and fantasy, favorite Disney characters come to life in incredible shows and attractions celebrating stories and legends familiar to all.

MAGIC KINGDOM PARK®

MAIN STREET, U.S.A.®

The Magic Kingdom experience begins with a nostalgic trip down Main Street, U.S.A., a fantasy version of small towns in America nearly a hundred years ago during the optimistic era of Walt Disney's boyhood. The old-time barbershop, ice cream parlor, ornate cinema, and wood-planked general store along the gingerbread Victorian street evoke a time when life had a simpler, easier pace.

Opposite, premiering October, 2001, 100 Years of Magic are celebrated in the Share A Dream Come True Parade down Main Street, U.S.A., where beloved Disney characters appear on floats that resemble giant snow globes.

COMING AND GOING

Children delight in the leisurely ride aboard a horse-drawn trolley pulled by powerful Percherons and Belgians. The quaint trolleys share Main Street, U.S.A. with other vehicles too: motorized jitneys (whose special mufflers create the appropriate sputtering sound of turn-of-the-century vehicles) and a scarlet fire engine, all traveling from Town Square to Cinderella Castle and back again. Or you can board one of four locomotives at the Main Street Train Station for a tour of the park.

SHOPPING

Behind the Victorian-era store-fronts there's everything from fine clothing to monogrammed Mouse ears and other souvenirs. Guests may be tempted by the aroma of fresh-from-the-oven cookies in the bakery. Or they can stop to watch candy makers stirring a pot of peanut brittle in the Main Street Confectionery, or a glass-blower crafting wares.

TOWN SQUARE EXPOSITION HALL

Dining Out

The Crystal Palace

Inspired by San Francisco's Conservatory of Flowers, the ornate Crystal Palace Restaurant is a Magic Kingdom landmark. Guests dine in a glass-ceilinged atrium amidst seasonal flowers and hanging greenery, with favorite Disney characters visiting tableside at breakfast, lunch, and dinner. The all-you-can-eat-buffet is a favorite for all ages.

The elaborate Town Square Exposition Hall located on the east side of Town Square is one of the first buildings guests encounter as they enter Magic Kingdom Park. A life-size sculpture of Goofy, right, tips his hat at the front door. The fanciful Victorian gingerbread building takes visitors back to another era, with rocking chairs on the front porch for relaxing after a day in the park.

THE HUB

Mickey Mouse stands hand in hand with Walt Disney at the end of Main Street, U.S.A., the departure point for seven magical lands. The bronze work of art, entitled "Partners," was dedicated in June 1995. The quote by Walt Disney at the base of the statue reads "We believe in our idea: a family park where parents and children could have fun together." The miniature sculptures of favorite Disney animated characters—Donald Duck, Minnie Mouse, Pinocchio, Dumbo, Goofy, and Pluto—encircle the gardens in Central Plaza, better known as the Hub.

"Partners"

ADVENTURELAND®

Strolling beneath dense vines and bamboo branches, guests make their way to Adventureland, where exotic locales—Southeast Asia, Africa, Polynesia, and the Caribbean—are combined into one colorful fantasy. Guests can explore the Swiss Family Treehouse, board a tropical launch for the popular Jungle Cruise, or be immersed in a great swashbuckling adventure in Pirates of the Caribbean.

Right, animated totem poles from The Enchanted Tiki Room—Under New Management entertain guests with a comical routine. Opposite page, hippos give a wide-mouthed greeting to adventurers on the Jungle Cruise, a trip inspired by waterways from the Egyptian Nile to Cambodia's Mekong.

JUNGLE CRUISE

Abandoned temples inspired by
ruins in Southeast Asia,
right, set the stage on
the Jungle Cruise, one
of the best-loved
rides in the Magic
Kingdom. It's a fan-
ciful journey by
canopied boat to
faraway places.
Awaiting guests at
every turn are fierce
tigers, curious gorillas,
playful elephants, and
frolicking hippos—all the work
of Disney's imaginative artists.

THE MAGIC CARPETS OF ALADDIN

Beside the newly constructed ancient Agrabah Bazaar, it's a whole new world of fun as The Magic Carpets of Aladdin send guests whirling around a large Genie lamp. The flying carpets are controlled by their riders as passengers decide on the side to side and tilt movements. Be sure to avoid the surrounding water-spitting camels!

SWISS FAMILY TREEHOUSE

This gigantic plant is the make-believe home of the castaway Robinson clan from Disney's film *Swiss Family Robinson*. The tree is unofficially classified as *Disneyodendron eximus*, a genus that humorously translates as "out-of-the-ordinary Disney tree." Weighing in at 200 tons, the fantastic tree is made of steel and concrete, and enlivened with 800,000 fabricated leaves, flowers, and buds. The tree showcases a fascinating pulley system, which uses bamboo buckets and a waterwheel to provide water high up in the branches. Visitors can climb the narrow stairs and peek in the study, bedrooms, a family room with a pump organ, and the spacious kitchen.

THE ENCHANTED TIKI ROOM— UNDER NEW MANAGEMENT

This newly transformed attraction features two stars from beloved Disney animated features: Iago, from *Aladdin*, and Zazu, from *The Lion King*, who play the new landlords in a witty, upbeat show. Longtime stars Michael, Pierre, Fritz, and José still appear, along with more than 225 birds, flowers, and tiki statues singing up a storm.

Did You Know?

The Enchanted Tiki Room, which opened at Disneyland Park in California in 1963, was the first attraction to feature Audio-Animatronics characters. The dozens of parrots, toucans, macaws, and other birds are created with mechanical, electrical, and hydraulic actions, all cued to a tape with show voices and music.

PIRATES OF THE CARIBBEAN

Guests are in for a great swashbuckling adventure when they pass through a battered fort to climb aboard boats for a watery journey. The fun begins with a passage through dark and mysterious grottos, followed by a dip down a waterfall and into the middle of a ferocious pirate battle for control of a harbor town. Spirited music and non-stop plundering and frolicking—including drunken pigs, barking dogs, and raucous pirates firing pistols and being chased by women—make this attraction one of the most popular in the Magic Kingdom Park.

FRONTIERLAND®

Step back into the land of frontier America—the old West with its boardwalks, brass-railed saloons, forts, and desertlike landscaping. The tallest Magic Kingdom peak—Splash Mountain—is here, as well as jagged Big Thunder Mountain Railroad. And youngsters can run free on Tom Sawyer Island, a low-tech oasis in the middle of the Magic Kingdom Park.

Big Thunder Mountain Railroad towers in the distance as the Walt Disney World Railroad makes a stop in Frontierland.

BIG THUNDER MOUNTAIN RAILROAD

Big Thunder Mountain Railroad, "the wildest ride in the wilderness," flies in a continuous string of dips and curves around the attraction's rugged red rocks. Riders speed past steaming volcanic lakes and bubbling phosphorescent pools, beneath waterfalls, and through the flooded mining town of Tumbleweed where gold diggers are having one last celebration before moving on to drier land. It took two years and 650 tons of steel to build the 197-foot mountain.

DIAMOND HORSESHOE SALOON REVUE

It's a hand-clappin', foot-stompin' good time in the horseshoe-shaped Dixieland Hall. The energetic show—with its mix of flashy cancan girls, singing cowboys, and corny jokes—is one of the best live performances in the Magic Kingdom. The attraction is based on the original Golden Horseshoe Revue, which opened at Disneyland Park in 1955.

FRONTIERLAND SHOOTIN' ARCADE

A cowboy town in the 1800s, complete with hotel, bank, jail, and cemetery, is the elaborate setting for this arcade. The .54-caliber buffalo rifles shoot infrared beams at targets with humorous results: a ghost rider gallops when a cloud is hit; a shot on the grave-digger's shovel makes a skull pop out of the grave.

Did You Know?

When the Frontierland Shootin' Arcade first opened in Magic Kingdom Park, sharpshooters used air guns that fired lead pellets—and the place required a fresh paint job every single night!

COUNTRY BEAR JAMBOREE

Lifelike bears sing, crack jokes, and spin tall tales in Grizzly Hall, just as they have for more than a quarter of a century. Favorites like Teddi Barra and the lovable Big Al keep the crowds giggling and tapping their toes through seasonal shows.

TOM SAWYER ISLAND

Take a raft across the Rivers of America to Tom Sawyer Island, a woodsy retreat with caves to explore, hills to climb, an old-fashioned swing bridge, and a fort with air guns that youngsters love to aim at passing riverboats. The slowly turning waterwheel on Harper's Mill sets the laid-back pace on this low-key island oasis. Relaxing grown-ups can often be found sipping lemonade on the front porch of Aunt Polly's Dockside Inn.

SPLASH MOUNTAIN®

Guests board hollowed-out logs to follow B'rer Bear, B'rer Fox, and B'rer Rabbit on a whimsical, watery journey to B'rer Rabbit's "laughin' place." Inspired by sequences and characters from the animated 1946 film *Song of the South*, Splash Mountain winds through swamps and bayous and culminates with a thrilling, 50 foot plunge at a 45 degree angle into the "briar patch," where riders are almost assured of getting splashed.

LIBERTY SQUARE

Welcome to the days of Colonial America in Liberty Square. Wide waterfront sidewalks, charming clapboard shops with brilliant flowers in window boxes, and the sounds of a riverboat help set the stage. The centerpiece is the majestic Liberty Tree, a live oak decorated with 13 lanterns to represent the original 13 colonies.

Right, The Haunted Mansion boasts 999 ghosts—but there's always room for one more! Opposite page, in the shadow of a giant oak known as the Liberty Tree, the distinctive Federal-style moldings of the Hall of Presidents evoke the spirit of America.

THE HALL OF PRESIDENTS

All 43 chief executives are on stage in this patriotic attraction, but only Abraham Lincoln and George W. Bush have speaking roles. The detailed research of Disney designers provided the images the sculptors used in creating the figures.

George W. Bush scheduled to debut at The Hall of Presidents Fall 2001

LIBERTY BELLE RIVERBOAT

Churning through the Rivers of America, the triple-decker riverboat *Liberty Belle* is a real steamboat, with a boiler that turns water to steam which drives the paddle wheel that propels the boat. Guests get a relaxing ride and great views of Liberty Square, Frontierland, and Tom Sawyer Island, while passing a landscape that evokes the Wild West.

LIBERTY TREE

Rooted in Liberty Square's courtyard, the Liberty Tree is the largest living thing in Magic Kingdom Park. The 135-year-old live oak is 40 feet high, 30 feet wide, and weighs 38 tons. As in Disney's film *Johnny Tremain*, 13 lanterns, each representing one of the original 13 colonies, hang from its branches.

THE HAUNTED MANSION

Take a spirited ride through a big old 18th-century mansion that comes alive with 999 ghosts and goblins. The dusty rooms are full of fantastic special effects, but perhaps most startling are the life-sized images floating to dance music in the formal dining room. As the spooky attraction comes to a close, a grinning ghoulie hitches a ride in every car.

FANTASYLAND®

The heart of Magic Kingdom Park is Fantasyland. It's the place Walt Disney dedicated to "all those children, young and old alike, who believe that dreams really can come true." Fairy tale architecture and attractions inspired by many of Disney's best-loved films and characters make this a memorable place for Disney fans of all generations.

Attractions such as Dumbo the Flying Elephant, opposite page, are among children's favorites. At right, this charming Cinderella fountain is tucked in a corner of Fantasyland near Cinderella Castle.

CINDERELLA CASTLE

Cinderella Castle, one of the most photographed sites in the world, evokes warm memories for millions of Walt Disney World guests. The spires soar to 189 feet, visible far beyond the theme park. The magical castle was inspired by several real European castles and palaces, and by the original designs for Disney's 1950 animated film classic Cinderella.

The story of Cinderella is depicted on five spectacular mosaic tile murals that line the castle's wide breezeway. The murals sparkle with more than 500 colors of jewel-like Italian glass, plus real silver and 14 karat gold. The visual delight is augmented by carved columns and hand-stitched medieval-style banners. The legend of the little cinder girl, her fairy godmother, and the prince culminates as guests step into Fantasyland. Cinderella's Golden Carrousel awaits just steps from the castle courtyard.

Dining Out

Cinderella's Royal Table

Cinderella's Royal Table is found up the castle's winding staircase. The room is elaborately designed with high ceilings, Gothic arches, stained-glass windows, and tapestry-backed chairs at heavy wooden tables. Servers dressed in medieval-style finery offer delicious fare at breakfast, lunch, and dinner. Best of all, Cinderella and her prince are often there to greet diners.

PETER PAN'S FLIGHT

Take a magical flight over the rooftops of London in fanciful pirate ships with Peter Pan, Tinker Bell, and the Darling children—Wendy, Michael, and John. Mr. Smee, Captain Hook, and other favorite characters from the 1953 classic animated film await in Never Land.

ARIEL'S GROTTO

Sculptures of Ariel and Sebastian beckon guests to the home of *The Little Mermaid*. Once in the colorful grotto, kids can meet Ariel and, surrounded by waterfalls, coral, and starfish, can pose for pictures and frolic in leapfrog fountains.

LEGEND OF THE LION KING

A young Simba is the star of this popular stage show, which uses elaborate puppets, music, and clips of the hit film to tell the story of *The Lion King*. Some of the giant puppets take up to four people to coordinate head, mouth, and feet movements, and are a delight for all ages. Special in-theater effects enhance the experience.

SNOW WHITE'S SCARY ADVENTURES

Children love this tale of Snow White's perilous journey through the forest, carefully watching for the Wicked Witch who makes several appearances throughout the attraction. Inspired by the classic 1937 film, the story ends on a happy note, with Snow White and her prince waving farewell to the seven dwarfs.

Mad Tea Party

Riders control the speed in this swirling, whirling, giant, pastel-colored teacup experience. The attraction is drawn from a scene from the 1951 film *Alice in Wonderland*, in which the Mad Hatter and the March Hare give a tea party to celebrate an unbirthday.

Dumbo the Flying Elephant

Kids of all ages love a spin on Dumbo the Flying Elephant. The lovable elephant with the over-sized ears takes guests gliding far above Fantasyland. Timothy Mouse, Dumbo's faithful friend from the 1941 film classic, stands atop the hot-air balloon at the center of the circle of flying elephants.

IT'S A SMALL WORLD®

First conceived for the 1964–65 New York World's Fair, this attraction is legendary. Boats carry guests past nearly 300 singing dolls in native costumes from more than 100 regions of the world. The simple song that is repeated in different languages throughout the attraction is one of the best-known Disney tunes of all time.

THE MANY ADVENTURES OF WINNIE THE POOH

The adventures of everybody's favorite "chubby little cubby" come to life when guests join Pooh and friends, including Piglet, Eeyore, Gopher, Owl, Rabbit, Tigger, Kanga, and Roo, for a magical journey through a storybook page and into the Hundred Acre Wood. In an experience heightened by special effects and memorable music, guests are whisked in Hunny Pots through a Blustery Day, arriving at one honey of a party with the whole gang.

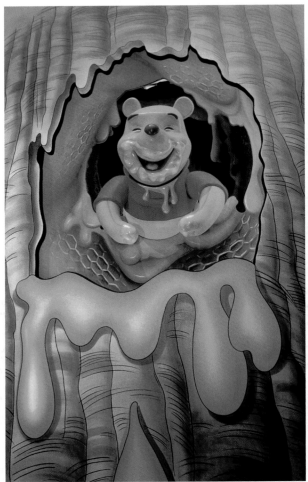

Cinderella's Golden Carrousel

This beautifully detailed antique masterpiece was originally built in 1917 and has been completely renovated. The eighteen panels above the horses show vividly colored, hand-painted scenes from the film *Cinderella*. Many of the 90 horses are original marvels of craftsmanship, and no two are alike.

THE SWORD IN THE STONE CEREMONY

Each day, Merlin the Magician chooses some lucky boy or girl to play the part of Arthur and pull the legendary sword Excalibur from the stone in front of Cinderella's Golden Carrousel. The sword will not budge for grown-ups, by the way.

Mickey's Toontown Fair®

Where is home, sweet home for beloved Disney characters? Mickey's Toontown Fair, the happy and friendly neighborhood where Mickey Mouse and Minnie Mouse await to invite children of all ages right into their homes. The whole land has a county fair ambience, with plenty of room for youngsters to roam and play.

Mickey greets guests in front of Mickey's Country House. Even the mailbox is a likeness of the world's most famous mouse. Opposite, town founder Cornelius Coot is honored with a whimsical statue in the middle of Mickey's Toontown Fair.

MICKEY'S COUNTRY HOUSE

Though the "Big Cheese" is away at work, the doors are always open to Mickey's Country House. Visitors get a glimpse of the clothes Mickey has neatly laid out on his bed; the Mickey Mouse cartoons playing on the television in the living room; the game room; and an old-fashioned kitchen. A comical trophy fish still on the line, below, hangs on his wall. Just outside the back door is Mickey's fanciful vegetable garden, where all the produce sprouts mouse ears.

MINNIE'S COUNTRY HOUSE

Kids are welcome to climb on the over-sized living room furniture in Minnie's pastel pink and purple world. Her kitchen is interactive—visitors can listen to an answering machine that plays Minnie's phone messages, open the refrigerator and check out the cheese-chip ice cream, or turn on the oven for a sweet surprise. And Minnie is sometimes found greeting guests in her backyard gazebo.

THE BARNSTORMER AT GOOFY'S WISE ACRES

The Barnstormer, the first kid-sized roller coaster at Walt Disney World Resort, is great fun for kids of all ages. The crazy adventure begins at Goofy's Wise Acres Farm, where real crops like tomatoes and corn grow right in the middle of the theme park. Since there's no height requirement, riders of all sizes can climb into crop dusters for a wild flight before crashing through the hayloft of Goofy's barn.

DONALD'S BOAT

Donald Duck has docked his boat, the *Miss Daisy*, providing splashing surprises for seafaring youngsters. A cross between a tugboat and a leaky ocean liner, Donald's yellow and red yacht features a twisted smokestack and a laundry line in a "pond" in which lily pads spout jumping streams and spray without warning. Inside, pint-sized seafarers can blow the boat's whistle or clang the *Miss Daisy*'s loud boat bell.

TOMORROWLAND®

Welcome to this neighborhood of sky-piercing beacons and glistening metal that looks like a city imagined by sci-fi writers and moviemakers of the 1920s and 1930s. Tomorrowland is a fantasy world where planet-hopping rocket ships battle space aliens and time-machine travel becomes a thrilling reality.

Rockets twirl and an elevated train glides by overhead in Tomorrowland, reopened in 1994 after an extensive redesign in which new attractions were added and existing ones revamped. There's great attention to design detail on the Avenue of the Planets, opposite, the grand entry to this fantasy city.

ASTRO ORBITER

The Astro Orbiter—a tower glowing with rings of flashing, changing colors—spins in the center of Tomorrowland, looking more like a comic book spacecraft than a 1990s space shuttle. Guests board the open-cockpit rockets for a tame trip through space—and a nice view of the surrounding Magic Kingdom lands.

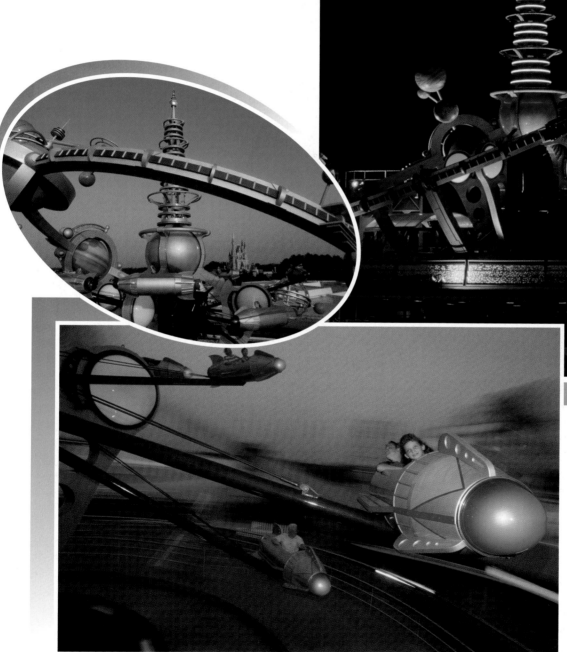

BUZZ LIGHTYEAR'S SPACE RANGER SPIN

Guests jump right in and join Buzz on an interactive adventure to defend the universe from the evil Emperor Zurg. To save the universe and collect points, riders blast orange-colored targets that trigger animation, sound, and light effects. Each space cruiser comes with turbocharged twin laser cannons and a joystick that is capable of spinning the craft 360 degrees.

SPACE MOUNTAIN®

Blast off into the night sky for a twisting, diving flight aboard the miniature space shuttles in this Magic Kingdom classic, still the ultimate thrill ride for millions of Walt Disney World guests. The journey begins as riders are thrust through a tunnel of flashing strobe lights and into the inky darkness for one of the most imaginative rides of their lives.

SUNNY ECLIPSE

He's one stylin' lounge lizard, and Sunny Eclipse never leaves the stage at Cosmic Ray's Starlight Cafe, the largest fast-food spot in the Magic Kingdom Park. Sunny, the story goes, is from the planet Zork, but now he's working for Cosmic Ray here on Earth—accompanied by his backup singers, the Space Angels.

WALT DISNEY'S CAROUSEL OF PROGRESS

Carousel of Progress is housed in a Disney-designed circular pavilion of 34,000 square feet, with six 240-seat theaters. The outer rim of the building, which seats the audience, rotates around the core of stages where the show is presented. Conceived by Walt Disney himself, the attraction was seen by more than 17 million visitors at the 1964–65 World's Fair, then opened in Disneyland Park in 1967.

Did You Know?

This historical show debuted at the 1964–65 New York World's Fair. It depicts the change in family life brought by electricity and inventions developed during the last 100 years. As the audience rotates past six stationary stages, characters representing a father, mother, son, and daughter interact with 20th-century technology. An updated final scene has been added that includes voice-activated systems, high-definition television, and virtual reality.

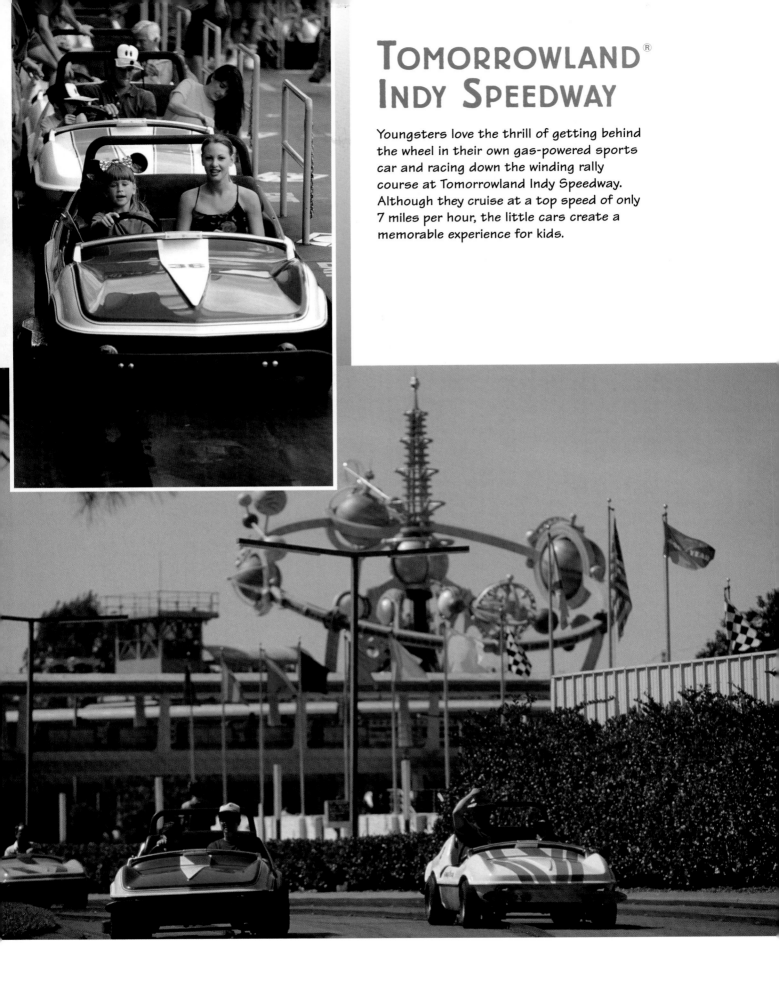

TOMORROWLAND®
INDY SPEEDWAY

Youngsters love the thrill of getting behind the wheel in their own gas-powered sports car and racing down the winding rally course at Tomorrowland Indy Speedway. Although they cruise at a top speed of only 7 miles per hour, the little cars create a memorable experience for kids.

THE TIMEKEEPER

A fantastic time-travel machine takes guests on a humorous whirlwind trip through time and space, hosted by The Timekeeper, a tinsel-haired mad scientist robot. His assistant is 9-Eye, inset above, a personable robot camera who flies through history and transmits footage back to the audience. The trip, created with a Circle-Vision 360 film and special in-theater effects, sweeps from the days of Leonardo da Vinci and Mozart to the 1900 Paris Exposition where the audience meets up with Jules Verne and H. G. Wells.

THE ExtraTERRORestrial ALIEN ENCOUNTER

An angry alien creature is accidentally beamed to Earth, and the catastrophic result is the story of The ExtraTERRORestrial Alien Encounter, providing the most frightening thrills of any Magic Kingdom attraction. The show, with its incredible in-theater special effects, plays on the audience's own fears and imaginations to create a chaotic and truly emotional experience.

NIGHT TIME MAGIC

The Vacation Kingdom lights up in dazzling colors after the sun goes down, from the twinkling Electrical Water Pageant, below, that floats along nightly on Bay Lake, and the Fantasy in the Sky Fireworks spectacular in the skies over Magic Kingdom Park. The SpectroMagic Parade has returned, featuring favorite Disney characters illuminated by thousands of shimmering fiber-optic lights moving in concert with a soaring musical score. Mickey Mouse, inset, works his magic over a crystal ball filled with over a hundred tiny lightning bolts.

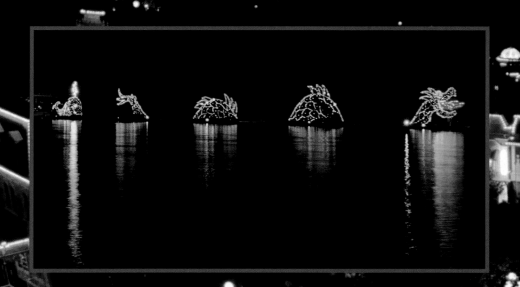

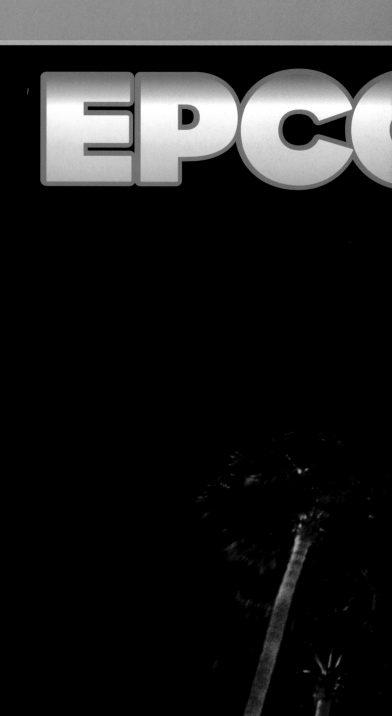

Epcot® combines Disney fun and imagination with the wonders of the real world, inspiring guests to discover things they did not know before. It's really two parks in one—Future World, featuring the newest and most intriguing ideas in science and technology, and World Showcase, celebrating the richness and diversity of world cultures.

FUTURE WORLD®

Whether it's a fantastic journey through the human body or a tire-squealing spin in a race car, Future World brings guests face-to-face with scientific achievements and 21st century technologies. The beautifully designed pavilions provide a wonderfully imaginative and entertaining look at transportation, communication, sea life, energy, agriculture, and the human body.

SPACESHIP EARTH

Guests take a fascinating journey through the history of human communication as they spiral to the top of the 180 foot high Spaceship Earth geosphere. Historic tableaus trace the development of language from caveman days through Egyptian, Greek, and Renaissance cultures, to the invention of the telegraph, telephone, television, and other current telecommunications systems. The days of the Roman Empire, right, and Gutenberg's printing press, opposite page top right, are two of the most detailed scenes. At the summit, there is a majestic star field and a look at future technologies as you pivot around for a backward descent.

Spaceship Earth weighs 16 million pounds—more than three times that of a space shuttle fully fueled and ready for launch. The outer "skin" is made up of 11,324 aluminum-and-plastic-alloy triangles. Also, rainwater does not run off the sphere onto the ground—a gutter was developed to collect the water and funnel it into World Showcase Lagoon.

When the journey ends in Spaceship Earth, guests can stroll through the Global Neighborhood, above, and interact with emerging technologies such as voice-activated television sets and telephones with silly sound effects.

INNOVENTIONS®

This interactive playground is in the heart of Epcot® and offers guests exciting live shows, demonstrations, and hands-on displays. Disney combined its talent for imagination and storytelling with the advanced technologies of some of the best companies in the world to create the 50,000 square foot attraction, which turns "future shock" into "'future fascination."

UNIVERSE OF ENERGY

Guests encounter life-sized dinosaurs in an odyssey through the primeval world in the Universe of Energy. It's a humorous ride-through adventure intended to show the importance of our natural resources and how energy is produced. The mirrored, pyramid-shaped pavilion is one of the most technologically complex attractions at Epcot®. Guests ride in unique 30,000 pound traveling theater cars, which are guided along a very thin wire embedded in the concrete floor. Two acres of solar cells on the roof supply some of the pavilion's power.

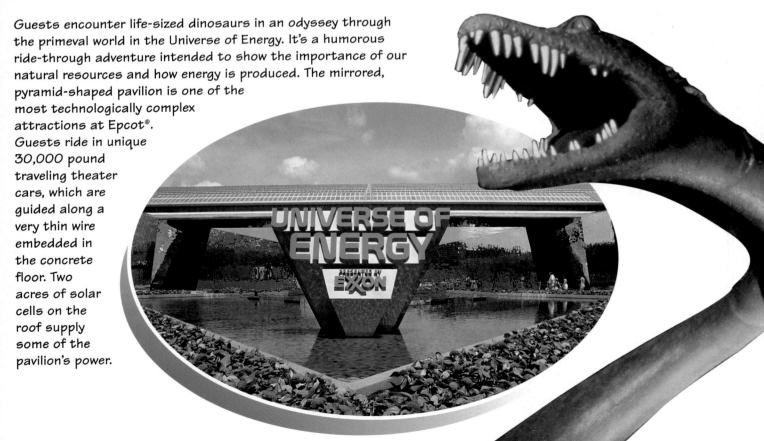

TEST TRACK

Climb into specially made cars for an exhilarating spin on Disney's longest, fastest thrill ride. Experience everything from a wildly out-of-control skid to a high-speed barrier test as the cars spiral and snake through areas simulating arctic cold and desert heat. The cars, powered by three onboard computers that together have more processing power than a space shuttle, hit speeds of 65 mph on the outdoor track—great fun for all ages.

WONDERS OF LIFE

The gleaming gold Wonders of Life pavilion takes both serious and amusing looks at health, fitness, and modern lifestyles. Body Wars, inset, thrills guests with a spectacular flight simulator adventure through the human body, combining the physical sensation of a roller coaster with terrific special effects film techniques. Cranium Command, right, is a humorous theater show in which the audience helps to pilot the brain of an adolescent boy.

IMAGINATION!

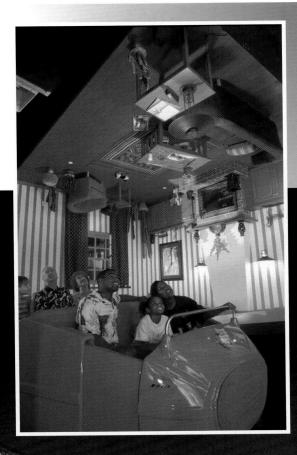

Oddly shaped mirrored glass pyramids house this pavilion, which features *Honey, I Shrunk the Audience.* This popular 3-D show, left, lets guests experience the feeling of shrinking, with some hilarious results. Journey Into Your Imagination, top right, combines special effects and optical illusions to change perceptions of the way people think and see the world, while Image Works, top left, is an interactive playground filled with imaginative activities.

THE LAND

Boats journey through lush greenhouses containing everything from papayas to cucumbers to cotton on a tour that takes a look at the history of farming and its future. Other attractions in the pavilion include Food Rocks!, a stage show with a zany cast of rock 'n' roll stars, such as rap artist Füd Wrapper, right, and The Excess, bottom, a trio of disheveled hard rockers. Circle of Life stars the cast of The Lion King in a beautiful environmental film.

THE LIVING SEAS

The world's largest saltwater tank is the centerpiece of The Living Seas, home to more than 3,000 sea creatures. Sharks, barracudas, parrot fish, rays, and dolphins make their home in a tank that is 200 feet in diameter and 27 feet deep, and holds 5.7 million gallons of water. Guests explore a model undersea-research facility at Sea Base Alpha, above. View the latest technologies in ocean surveillance and management in action, including robotic submersibles, space-age diving suits, and communications systems.

WORLD SHOWCASE®

Exotic cuisine, scenic wonders, artisans, and entertainment from eleven countries greet visitors to World Showcase. Gathered around a 40-acre lagoon beyond Future World, the buildings, streets, gardens, and monuments of each land are designed to give Epcot® guests an authentic experience. Native speakers act as friendly cultural ambassadors.

CANADA

Hôtel du Canada leads guests to the Canada pavilion, a mixture of rustic Native Indian villages, ornate French-flavored buildings, the Scottish heritage of the Maritimes, and the ruggedness of the Canadian Rockies. The pavilion introduces visitors to the traditions, cultures, and atmosphere of the places that draw most tourists to Canada.

Dining Out

Le Cellier

Tucked away near the Canadian Pavilion's Victoria Gardens, this stone-walled steakhouse has the cozy ambience of a wine cellar and offers traditional Canadian fare, including steaks, roast prime rib, and the longtime favorite, Canadian cheddar cheese soup. For diners who prefer fish, the maple-glazed salmon is a winner.

UNITED KINGDOM

Quaint cottages, lush flower gardens, and cobblestone streets take visitors back to merry Old England. You can stroll from an elegant London Square to the countryside in just a few short steps. The Toy Soldier, right, is among the delightful shops that offer everything from British toys to Scottish sweaters and delicate china dinnerware.

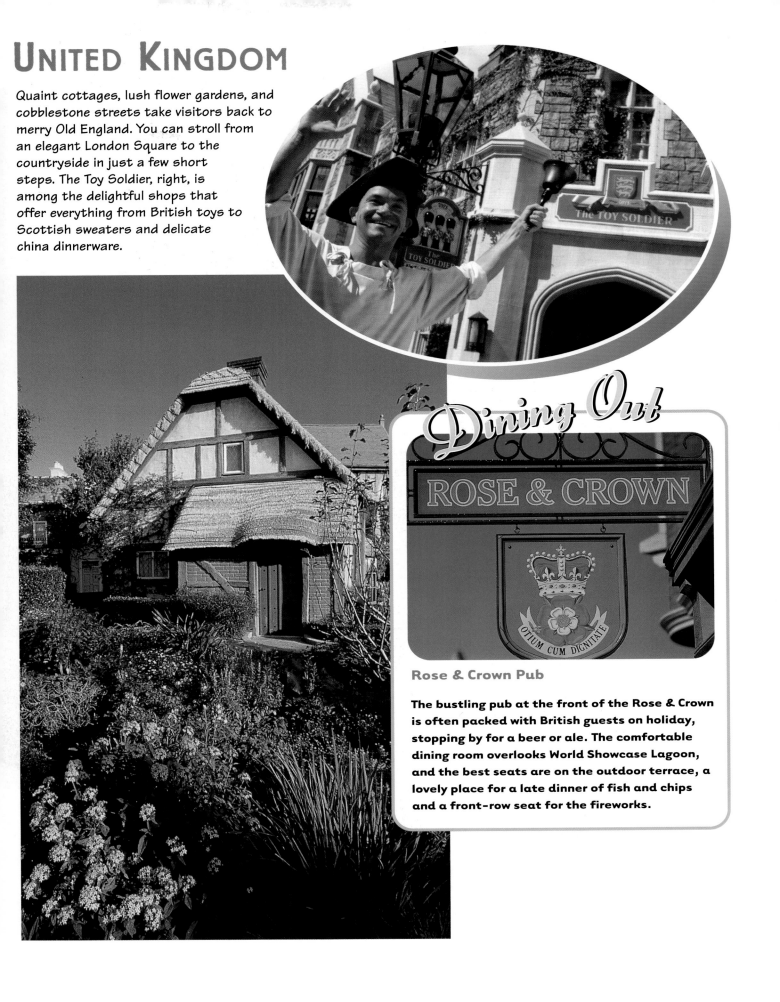

Dining Out

Rose & Crown Pub

The bustling pub at the front of the Rose & Crown is often packed with British guests on holiday, stopping by for a beer or ale. The comfortable dining room overlooks World Showcase Lagoon, and the best seats are on the outdoor terrace, a lovely place for a late dinner of fish and chips and a front-row seat for the fireworks.

FRANCE

Dining Out

Les Chefs de France

Millions of World Showcase visitors have been introduced to nouvelle cuisine at Les Chefs de France, created by three of the most renowned chefs in France — Paul Bocuse, Gaston Lenôtre, and Roger Vergé. The bright, airy restaurant is drenched in natural light and has the ambience of a popular Parisian bistro.

In the shadow of the Eiffel Tower, guests sample the beauty and charm of France and its people. Guests can visit shops selling perfume, wines, and other luxury items, or follow the heavenly aromas of the bake shop through streets bordered by distinguished buildings with copper and slate roofs, dormer windows, and intricate wrought iron.

MOROCCO

Dining Out

Restaurant Marrakesh

Behind its pink plaster facade, past arched columns and massive carved wooden doors, guests dine in an atmosphere typical of an elaborate southern Moroccan fortress. The menu features popular Moroccan dishes such as couscous, a flaky chicken pie called *bastilla*, and *tagine djaj belhamed*, stewed chicken in preserved lemons and olives. Adding to the experience, belly dancers, accompanied by a Moroccan musical ensemble, entertain diners.

The Koutoubia Minaret, right, the famous prayer tower in Marrakesh, stands guard over the entrance to this exotic North African land. Nine tons of colorful hand-cut tiles and 23 artisans were brought from Morocco to create the detailed work throughout the pavilion. The bustling marketplace, top inset, is stocked with imported handicrafts.

JAPAN

A bright red torii gate along the shoreline welcomes guests to centuries of Japanese culture. The blue-roofed Goju-no-to pagoda was inspired by a shrine in Nara built in A.D. 700. It looms above the entrance, topped by a bronze spire with gold wind chimes and a water flame. Guests can wander through pathways in perfectly groomed gardens before shopping in the famed Mitsukoshi department store.

Dining Out

Teppanyaki Dining Room

Sociable chefs put on a great show with their flashing knives as they chop and grill on giant *teppan* tabletops. The atmosphere is casual and relaxed. Diners sit counter-style around the grill while the skilled chefs chop meats, seafood, and vegetables at lightning speed to create a generous stir-fry that is shared with each guest at the table.

ITALY

Guests encounter Venetian red-and-white striped moorings and graceful gondolas on their stroll around World Showcase Lagoon. The slender Campanile rises above the piazza, a re-creation of St. Mark's Square in Venice. A replica of the 1309 Doge's Palace and Neptune's splashing fountain surround visitors in an authentic Italian atmosphere.

Dining Out

L'Originale Alfredo de Roma Ristorante

Fresh pasta rolls off the press just inside the entrance to Alfredo's, enticing diners to sample authentic Italian fare. Decorated in the warm earth tones characteristic of Florence and Siena, Alfredo's creates an inviting atmosphere in which to sample delicious pasta specialties, like their famous fettuccine Alfredo tossed with imported Parmesan cheese.

THE AMERICAN ADVENTURE

Celebrate America's history and diversity in The American Adventure, a patriotic journey through America's past, housed in a Georgian-style mansion. Stirring words from Benjamin Franklin begin this exploration of the American spirit, and the attraction features other Audio-Animatronics performers including Mark Twain, Thomas Jefferson, Frederick Douglass, Susan B. Anthony, Alexander Graham Bell, Teddy Roosevelt, Charles Lindbergh, and John F. Kennedy.

GERMANY

The statue honoring St. George, the patron saint of soldiers, rises in the plaza in the heart of Germany. Strolling accordian players, an oompah band, and yodelers create an atmosphere of conviviality. German legends and fairy tales inspired the architecture, a blend of towns in the Rhine region, Bavaria, and in the German north.

Dining Out

Biergarten

Prosit! is the word in the Biergarten. Diners toast to good health with mugs of beer, light or dark, and sample from an all-you-can-eat buffet of German sausages, homemade spaetzle, potato salad, and other German specialties. Revelers often join the lively Bavarian musicians on stage.

CHINA

Guests pass through the Gate of the Golden Sun to the opulent, three-tiered Temple of Heaven, which symbolizes the Chinese universe. The exquisite temple is surrounded by a meditation garden, where the strains of soothing traditional Chinese music linger in the air.

Dining Out

九龍飯館
Nine Dragons
restaurant

Nine Dragons Restaurant

Diners take an epicurean adventure into the Chinese provinces at Nine Dragons. Five cooking styles—Mandarin, Cantonese, Szechuan, Hunan, and Kiangche—are incorporated into the diverse menu, which offers everything from pan-fried dumplings to red bean ice cream, plus a selection of Chinese teas, beers, and wines.

NORWAY

The architectural styles of Bergen, Alesund, Oslo, and Setesdal are featured around the pavilion's cobblestone plaza. Inside, visitors join Maelstrom on a fantasy voyage that leaves from a modern-day Norwegian village, journeys up a cascading waterway, and passes into the shadows of a mythical Norwegian forest populated by trolls and water spirits.

Dining Out

Restauant Akershus

This authentic Norwegian dining experience begins with a tasty traditional *koltbord* of seafood and cold meat dishes. Next come the *smarvarmt*, or hot dishes, including fish, venison, smoked pork, and other native dishes. The beautiful dining room is designed with carved wood ceilings and Gothic archways.

MEXICO

A Mayan pyramid dominates the entrance to Mexico, expressing the proud pre-Columbian heritage of the country. Inside is a gallery of artifacts from throughout Mexico's history. Near the gallery, a festival atmosphere prevails at a typical Colonial plaza. Beyond the plaza, guests begin a boat journey for a look at the colorful heritage and attractions of Mexico.

Dining Out

San Angel Inn

The emphasis is on authentic Mexican cuisine. The house specialty is *mole poblano*, a chicken dish with a rich sauce made of cocoa, chile ancho, chile passilla, green tomatoes, ground tortillas, coriander seed, and 11 other spices.

Tapestry of Dreams

Tapestry of Dreams features towering puppets and colorful floats in a jubilant, kinetic street party of sight, sound, and imagination. More than 150 puppeteers and performers travel along the World Showcase Promenade in a musical cavalcade complete with primal percussion and tribal dances. The puppets, in 40 different designs, are the creations of artist Michael Curry, award-winning designer for *The Lion King* on Broadway.

Tapestry of Dreams parade scheduled to premiere October, 2001

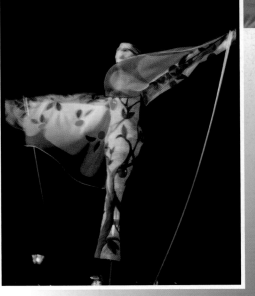

IllumiNations: Reflections of Earth

The nighttime sky above World Showcase Lagoon erupts with bursting fireworks and laser tracings in IllumiNations: Reflections of Earth, which celebrates our world in a spectacular extravaganza of fire and light. This one-of-a-kind entertainment presents the entire history of our planet from its creation to the present and a look towards the future with a dazzling mix of special effects, full-color lasers, brilliant fireworks, water fountains, and fiery torches.

The technically complex show requires 67 computers in 40 key locations, hundreds of special lighting fixtures, a fountain barge that pumps 5,000 gallons of water a minute, and an inferno barge with 37 nozzles shooting propane flames in the air. Every explosion of fireworks is timed to the beat of an original symphonic score that is a blend of ethnic rhythms and melodies from around the world.

Immerse yourself in the glitz and excitement of show business at the Disney-MGM Studios. Broadway-style shows, backstage glimpses, and spectacular attractions celebrate the public's ongoing love affair with movies, television, and music at "the Hollywood that never was and always will be." And beginning on October 1, 2001, the Disney-MGM Studios is the center of the Walt Disney World Resort 100 Years of Magic Celebration, as seen opposite in the Opening Ceremonies.

EARFFEL TOWER

No Hollywood movie studio lot would be complete without a water tower, but at Disney-MGM Studios, it couldn't be just any water tower. "Earffel Tower," as it's playfully referred to, sports a pair of 5,000 pound mouse ears.

THE GREAT MOVIE RIDE

Some of the most famous films in silver screen history come to life in The Great Movie Ride. Guests ride through spectacular scenes from some of their favorite movies, and witness a grand finale film montage. The attraction calls to mind images of the many legendary film stars who have left their stellar performances in the Hollywood firmament.

FANTASMIC!

The brilliant Fantasmic! spectacular features 50 performers and combines dazzling special effects, colorful pyrotechnics, beloved Disney characters, animation, and dancing waters synchronized to the melodies of timeless Disney classics. The show takes place inside the dreams of Mickey Mouse. When Disney villains intrude on Mickey's fantasy and turn his dreams into nightmares, Mickey uses the power of good to triumph over evil. His magic creates shooting comets, swirling stars, balls of fire, and other amazing wonders. Staged in a 6,500-seat amphitheater off Sunset Boulevard, Fantasmic! uses nearly 2 million gallons of water to create many of the special effects.

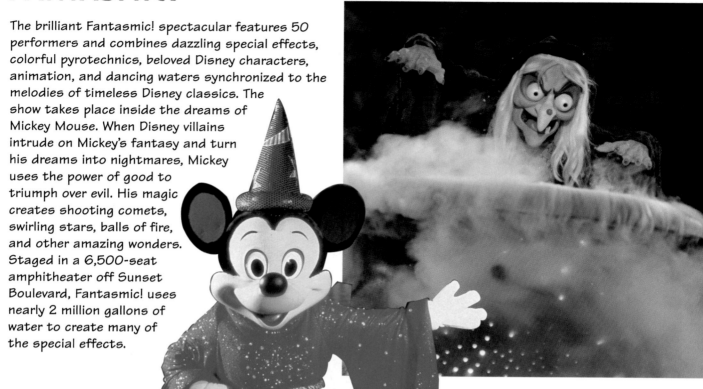

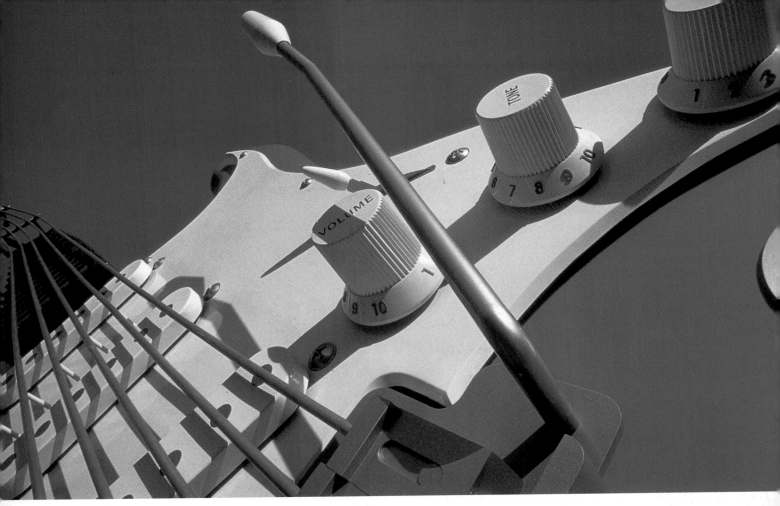

Rock 'n' Roller Coaster® Starring Aerosmith

Rock 'n' Roller Coaster Starring Aerosmith blasts from 0 to 60 mph in 2.8 seconds, and guests encounter nearly 5 Gs as they transition from launch to loop at the ride's first inversion. The thrilling trip in stretch-limo trains features three complete inversions, with the wild twists and turns amplified by a specially recorded Aerosmith soundtrack that resonates out of 125 speakers in each train on the indoor coaster.

THE MAGIC OF DISNEY ANIMATION

Disney fans get an inside look at the way classic animated films are created in this enlightening tour of the Florida animation studios. Visitors get to see the talented animators working at their drafting tables and creating the drawings that will come to life in upcoming Disney films. For a 24-minute film, the studio's 70-plus animators produce 34,650 drawings with at least 300 background scenes.

Canopied shuttles take guests behind the scenes for a look at television and movie production, from seamstresses at work on costumes to an exciting and up-close look at special effects. The shuttle cruises by the familiar skyline of New York City, above, rendered on painted flats. Below, on the walking portion of the backlot tour, one lucky guest is chosen to demonstrate special effects—and gets doused with 400 gallons of water!

VOYAGE OF THE LITTLE MERMAID

Disney's blockbuster animated film *The Little Mermaid* comes to life in an underwater musical featuring the villainous Ursula, below, trying to steal Ariel's lovely melodious voice. Prince Eric makes an appearance, as well as Flounder and Sebastian, who are brought to life by puppeteers. The show combines animation, live action, and special effects, including an intense lightning storm. The tale ends happily, of course, with a sensational grand finale.

BEAUTY AND THE BEAST— LIVE ON STAGE

This musical extravaganza tells the mesmerizing fairy tale love story of Belle and the Beast, including all the action, humor, and romance that made the animated film a hit. The show borrows many of the film's most popular songs, opening with the joyous *Be Our Guest*, and concluding with Belle and her prince dancing, far right, to the theme song *Beauty and the Beast*. They are surrounded by dazzling special effects, white doves, and serenading lords and ladies.

DISNEY'S THE HUNCHBACK OF NOTRE DAME— A MUSICAL ADVENTURE

Gypsies retell the story of the bell ringer Quasimodo and his quest for love and happiness in a colorful musical that takes place in 15th-century Paris. Clopin, the King of the Gypsies, narrates the fast-paced tale of the Hunchback and Esmeralda, describing their love story through song, masks, puppets, and dance. The exuberant show spills down runway ramps and into the audience, and features toe-tapping tunes from the hit film, including *Topsy Turvy* and *A Guy Like You.*

JIM HENSON'S MUPPET*VISION 3D

Adjusting their 3-D glasses, guests sit back for a hilarious immersion into the zany world of the rambunctious Muppets. The audience is invited to the Muppet Labs, where Kermit the Frog is host for a show that applies Disney's Audio-Animatronics to extraordinary 3-D technology. The wild experience is enhanced by some amazing in-theater effects—floating bubbles, squirting boutonnieres, high winds, and a cannon blast.

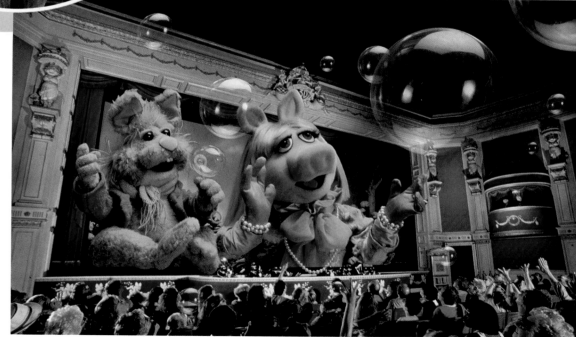

STAR TOURS

The experience begins as guests encounter a battle-disabled Imperial Walker looking down on the treetop homes of the Ewoks. Inside, riders buckle up for a wild galactic journey aboard a careening StarSpeeder 3000 spacecraft to the Moon of Endor, a thrill-a-second experience that combines flight simulator technology with an action-packed motion picture.

INDIANA JONES™ EPIC STUNT SPECTACULAR

Highly trained stunt performers brave earth-shattering crashes and fiery explosions to thrill the audience with a backstage view of moviemaking. Actors performing in an outdoor amphitheater re-create scenes from the blockbuster films to demonstrate how Hollywood can trick moviegoers into thinking a favorite celebrity has been punched or shot or has taken a fall.

Who Wants To Be A Millionaire-Play It! begins when the guest with the fastest finger is chosen from the audience to land in the "hot seat" and play for prizes as the popular game show is brought to life in all its suspenseful spectacle. Players still have three lifelines for help, but when guests "phone a friend," the call will go to a complete stranger who happens to be passing by outside the theater.

Drew Carey as an undercover cop?

Sounds Dangerous

SOUNDS DANGEROUS STARRING DREW CAREY

Comedian Drew Carey stars in *Sounds Dangerous*, a hair-raising demonstration of sensory sound effects at the ABC Sound Studios. As Carey is "filming" an action-packed TV pilot detective show, the picture is lost and the audience must follow a chase using binaural-sound headphones. Angry bees, a herd of galloping elephants, and a high-speed auto race are just a few of the sensational sound effects guests experience in the darkened theater.

HONEY, I SHRUNK THE KIDS MOVIE SET ADVENTURE

There is plenty of room for kids to stretch on this giant backyard playground inspired by the hit film *Honey, I Shrunk the Kids*. Huge blades of grass stretch 30 feet above the soft surface, and youngsters can climb on colossal insects and spiderwebs, explore caves, or slide down an oversized piece of film.

DINING AT THE STUDIOS

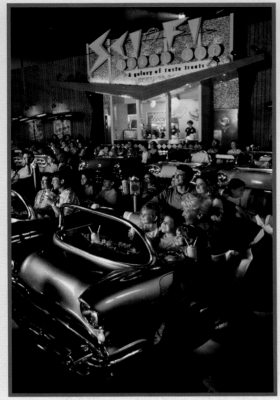

One of the most popular themed restaurants at the Disney-MGM Studios is the upscale Hollywood Brown Derby, above and right, where the famed Cobb Salad is still made from the original recipe.

The 50s Prime Time Cafe, above and center, is straight out of a black-and-white TV sitcom, with a menu that focuses on delicious comfort foods.

At the Sci-Fi Dine-In Theater, top left, the tables are re-creations of 1950s cars and the restaurant is a darkened drive-in movie set. A large screen shows some of the best and worst sci-fi trailers and cartoons from the 50s while guests munch on sandwiches, salads, and tempting desserts.

Mama Melrose's Ristorante Italiano, left, fires up the wood-burning oven to create crispy pizzas. Mama Melrose welcomes guests to her cozy eatery and often stops by the table to check on the chef's special lasagna, chicken, veal, and pasta dishes.

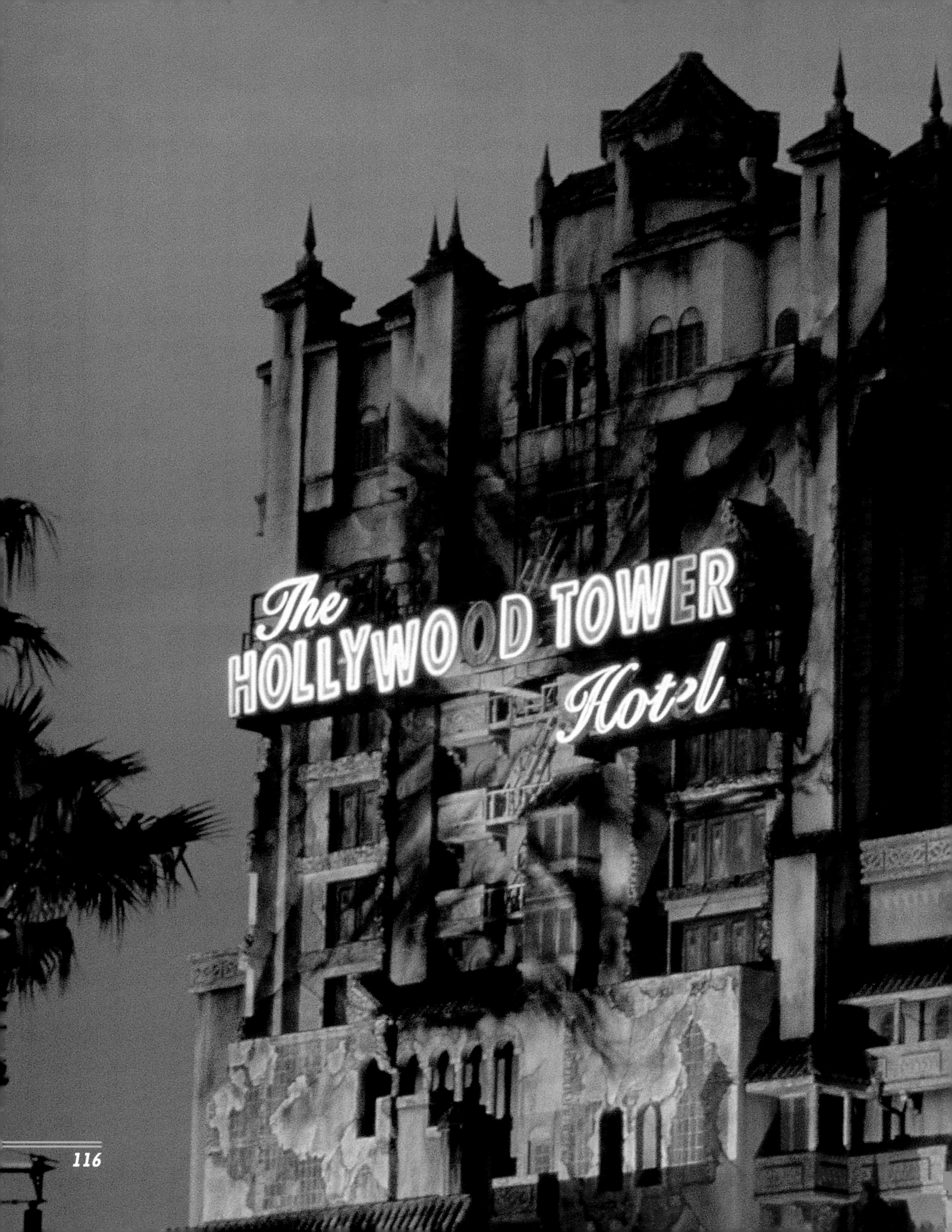
The
HOLLYWOOD TOWER
Hotel

Even more terror has been added to the faster-than-free-fall plunge from the 13th story of the abandoned Hollywood Tower hotel at the end of Sunset Boulevard. The terror begins when visitors board a decrepit "freight elevator" that slowly rises past mysterious hotel passageways, then passes through the Fifth Dimension to enter a pitch-black shaft for the gut-wrenching drop. Riders rise to the top of the tower at breathtaking speeds, then drop to the bottom not once, but a surprising two or sometimes three times - more drops than ever before.

Disney's imaginative stories come to life in new ways in this extraordinary theme park that was inspired by an endless fascination with animals. In a lush and verdant setting, paths and trails lead into five lands of adventure. Here you can encounter ferocious dinosaurs, behold thousands of wild creatures, and find favorite Disney characters.

THE OASIS

This cool, natural gateway introduces Disney's Animal Kingdom Theme Park, lush with flowering glades and tumbling water-falls. Winding paths lead to natural animal habitats for miniature deer, brilliant macaws, iguanas, tree kangaroos, an anteater, and other fascinating creatures.

DISCOVERY ISLAND™

An island village of brilliantly colored shops and restaurants is at the center of Disney's Animal Kingdom Theme Park. More than 50 artisans from the island of Bali worked for nearly two years to produce hundreds of folk art carvings featured on the buildings, a fusion of world folk art that includes pre-Columbian, Peruvian, African, and Polynesian styles.

TREE OF LIFE

The giant Tree of Life rises 14 stories into the sky, its leafy canopy spreading across the vast landscape. The giant roots twist over and into the earth, melding with a quiet landscape of pools, meadows, and trees that provides a natural habitat for flamingos, otters, lemurs, deer, tortoises, and kangaroos.

Carved into the tree's gnarled roots and mighty trunk is a rich tapestry of more than 300 animals, from the mighty lion to the playful dolphin. Its 103,000 leaves were attached by hand to the more than 8,000 branches. The artistry of the tree, with its detailed carvings and composition, required 20 artists, who met the challenge of creating a work of art that was both natural and fantastic. The creation is considered one of the most impressive artistic and engineering feats ever designed by Disney.

It's Tough To Be a Bug!®

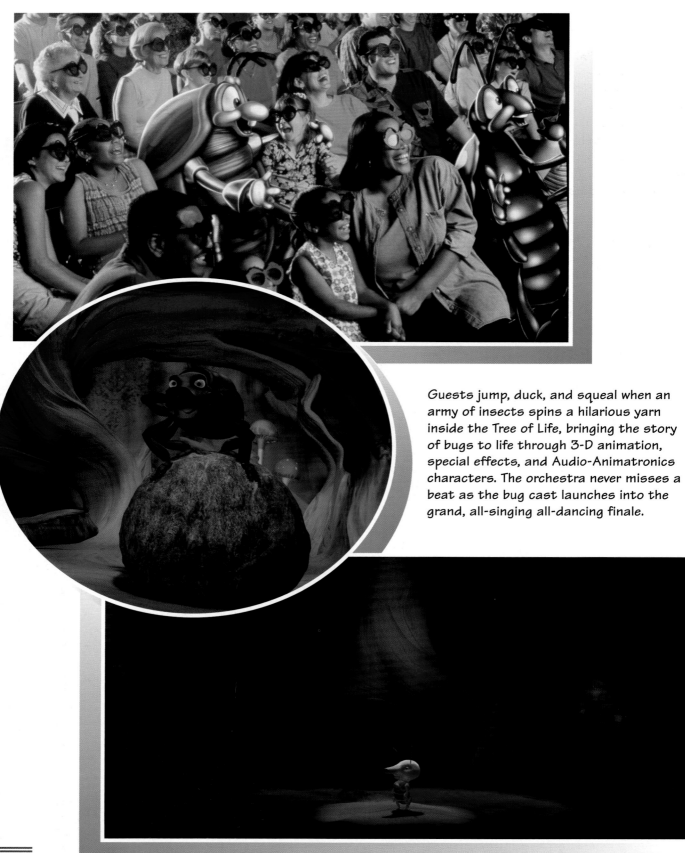

Guests jump, duck, and squeal when an army of insects spins a hilarious yarn inside the Tree of Life, bringing the story of bugs to life through 3-D animation, special effects, and Audio-Animatronics characters. The orchestra never misses a beat as the bug cast launches into the grand, all-singing all-dancing finale.

THE TREE OF LIFE GARDEN

The striking pink of a flock of flamingos provides a dramatic contrast to the rich greens and browns of the Tree of Life. Galapagos Tortoises, Blue-and-yellow macaws, and Red Kangaroos flourish in the lush vegetation of the Tree of Life Garden. Frolicking otters can be observed above ground, as well as through an underwater viewing area.

CAMP MINNIE-MICKEY

Mickey and Minnie await their friends at this Adirondack-style camp, a cool and leafy spot nestled in a Northeastern forest of cedar and birch trees. Other favorite characters often make appearances at meeting spots along the rustic hiking trail. Along with the Disney characters, Camp Minnie-Mickey is home to two live shows, one starring Pocahontas, and one starring Simba from *The Lion King*.

POCAHONTAS AND HER FOREST FRIENDS

At Grandmother Willow's Grove, Pocahontas helps guests discover the secret to saving America's forests and the creatures that live there. With Grandmother Willow's help and the participation of a live raccoon, skunk, possum, forest doves, and porcupines, Pocahontas and her guests learn that only humans can save the forest.

FESTIVAL OF THE LION KING

Standing ovations and rave reviews continue for Festival of the Lion King, an uplifting Broadway-style musical full of pageantry and spectacular floats. Simba, as well as other animal heroes of the hit animated film, joins energetic singers, dancers, and acrobatic performers, many costumed in resplendent African tribal garb.

AFRICA

The village of Harambe on the edge of Africa was inspired by the small East African coastal town of Lamu, Kenya. Designers chose not to copy a single street or marketplace, but to capture the essence of its coral-walled buildings, thatched roofs, and narrow winding streets—a romantic backdrop for the exciting realism of the African safari.

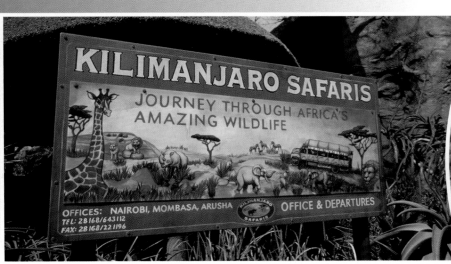

Walt Disney Imagineers made countless trips to Africa to collect native artifacts, distinctive signs, and designs to create a town that looks weathered by time. Additionally, 13 Zulu craftspeople were brought to Florida to make the thatched huts in the village and Tusker House Restaurant. Harambe, which means "come together," is the starting point for Kilimanjaro Safaris, and the dining and shopping center of Disney's Animal Kingdom's Africa.

KILIMANJARO SAFARIS® EXPEDITION

Guests catch a ride in all-terrain, open-sided trucks for an adventure across the broad savanna where animals are just inches from the truck, living under trees, wallowing in waterholes, and grazing in the tall grasses. Along the way, the guide gives information about the journey and about the great dangers threatening the world's wild animal population.

Creatures great and small live naturally in the broad grasslands and green forests, where only invisible barriers keep the animals separated for peaceful coexistence. The safari show turns dramatic when an elephant is "wounded" and a baby elephant is missing. The bush pilot asks for help capturing a band of ivory poachers, and a wild chase begins.

PANGANI FOREST EXPLORATION TRAIL®

For an intimate walk with the animals, Pangani Forest Exploration Trail passes through lush jungle glades to reach the adventurous heart of the land of Africa. The trail begins near the bustling riverfront village of Harambe, but civilization falls behind as guests pass under a thatched archway for a self-guided tour that allows a close-up study of animals, rare birds, fish, and reptiles. A curious okapi, below, a small antelope descended from the giraffe, pokes his long neck into view.

One of the most fascinating sights is the family of lowland gorillas, just inches away from the trail foraging through the trees and bushes. From a swaying suspension bridge, guests can observe the family—two young females, a silverback male, and a baby, below. In the other direction, a group of young male gorillas lives separately, participants in an unusual study of gorilla social habits. Meerkats, left, stand guard near the savanna over-look, a circular, thatched-roof structure with a grand view of the grasslands where giraffes as well as tiny dik-diks and other members of the antelope family are seen grazing in knee-high grass.

WILDLIFE EXPRESS®

The *Wildlife Express* runs from the village of Harambe to Rafiki's Planet Watch, giving guests the opportunity to travel by rail behind the scenes. The puffing steam engines, re-creations of those first produced 150 years ago, provide a nostalgic excursion. Passenger carriages are partly enclosed by louvered wood shutters, with carpet bags, boxes, crates, and wicker luggage stacked high on the weathered rooftops.

Visitors step off the *Wildlife Express* and walk down a leafy trail to Conservation Station at Rafiki's Planet Watch for a backstage look at how the park's animals are kept healthy and happy at the veterinary headquarters. The facility also serves as the center for Disney's Animal Kingdom conservation programs. Visitors enjoy interactive experiences and meet wildlife experts to discover how they can help endangered animals around the world. Outdoors, the Affection Section, below and opposite, is the place to meet and touch fascinating animals.

ASIA

The mythical village of Anandapur, which translates as "place of delight," welcomes guests across the Asia Bridge. The village is filled with crumbling yet beautiful ruins, including a temple and maharajah's palace. Nepal, Thailand, and Indonesia are represented through architecture, animal carvings, and ruins throughout the village. Hundreds of wild creatures inhabit Anandapur, like the curious gibbons, bottom left, swinging from a Nepalese-styled monument tower to the ruins of a temple.

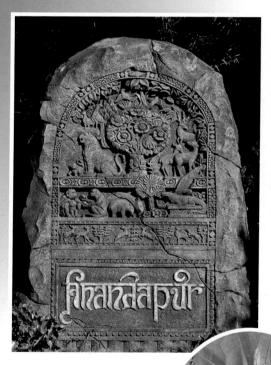

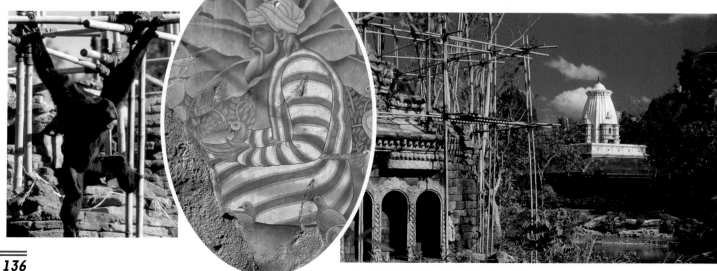

MAHARAJAH JUNGLE TREK

Asia reveals a natural treasure of wild creatures as you stroll along the path. Walk right up to the large open window overlooking the bat habitat and watch giant fruit bats fly above the cliffs of Anandapur or hang from the trees. Bottom, a curious tapir comes out for a look while a Komodo dragon, far right, the largest monitor lizard in the world (some grow to 12 feet long), suns nearby.

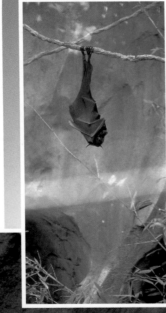

The magnificent tigers are a main attraction on the Maharajah Jungle Trek. From the top of a parapet, through a stand of bamboo, or from a bridge that stands amid the ruins near a flourishing herb garden, you can see these exotic animals roaming and playing in the ruins of a giant tiger shrine.

138

FLIGHTS OF WONDER

This humorous show, set in a crumbling Asian fort, highlights the beauty and diversity of birds. It features macaws, ibis, and other birds that emerge from alcoves to soar overhead. Although the show is carefully rehearsed, the birds are taught to show off their natural talents, not to do tricks. Trainers demonstrate how birds respond to special audio or visual clues, how they hunt, and how they eat.

KALI RIVER RAPIDS®

A wild, wet ride on the Chakranadi River is in store for raft riders on this adventure through a jungle habitat jeopardized by illegal logging. Gliding beyond the wondrous rain forest and temple ruins, the raft begins to twist and spin, passing a logged-out forest burning wildly. Disaster, of course, is avoided, but there are surprises around every turn, including an unexpected drop into churning waters.

DinoLand U.S.A.®

The sculpted skeleton of a giant 50 foot tall brachiosaurus straddles the entrance to DinoLand U.S.A., a quaint and playful land that celebrates America's fascination with these giant creatures. Chester & Hester's Dinosaur Treasures, opposite bottom, recalls the roadside souvenir stops that stood along highways 50 years ago.

142

CHESTER & HESTER'S DINO-RAMA!

Those wacky dino-maniacs are at it again at Chester & Hester's Dino-Rama!, a cretaceously-crazy fun fair complete with midway games and rides. Play Ringosaurus, toss beanbags into the jaws of a dinosaur, or hold on tight on the giant toy top TriceraTop Spin and the Primeval Whirl coaster.

THE BONEYARD® DIG SITE

Youngsters dig into the past at The Boneyard, a rambling open-air dig site rich with bones, fossils, and reconstructed skeletons. The space provides plenty of enjoyable activities for children, who can climb, crawl, and slide through a discovery-oriented maze of skeletons of triceratops, Tyrannosaurus rex, and other giants of the dinosaur age.

Did You Know?

Near the entrance to Dinosaur is a full-scale replica of the largest and most complete Tyrannosaurus skeleton ever discovered. Named after the fossil hunter that found it, "Sue" is 42 feet long and stands 12 feet tall at the hip. The actual skeleton resides at the Field Museum in Chicago.

Tarzan™ Rocks!

Tarzan™ Rocks! brings the energy of the hit Disney film *Tarzan™* to life at Disney's Animal Kingdom in a high-flying extravaganza in Theater in the Wild. Three of the film's stars—Tarzan™, Jane, and Terk—join singers, dancers, gymnasts, aerialists, and in-line skaters on stage for the four-act show that features five songs from the film's soundtrack, including the hit single, "You'll Be in My Heart."

DINOSAUR

Board a Time Rover in this high-speed adventure and take a journey back 65 million years to the time when dinosaurs stalked primeval forests. While an asteroid powerful enough to wipe out life on Earth speeds closer and closer, riders are whisked through the fiery end of the Cretaceous period as they race to find and return with an iguanodon dinosaur. A hail of small meteors sends a warning that the asteroid is approaching—along with a monstrous, meat-eating carnotaurus. The chase is on!

The four theme parks are just the beginning of the fun. The magic continues 24 hours a day at Walt Disney World Resort. From fabulous themed resorts to rollicking, relaxing water parks and world-class shopping, entertainment, and dining, this is the most complete vacation destination in the world.

A World of Fun

DISNEY'S TYPHOON LAGOON®

Designed to look like a ramshackle island village with a wrecked boat stranded on its mountain peak, Disney's Typhoon Lagoon offers a cool getaway. Although the centerpiece is a giant surfing lagoon, twice the size of a football field, the most popular attraction is the Humunga Kowabunga water slide, which drops guests down the mountain at speeds up to 30 m.p.h. For a tamer adventure, Shark Reef brings snorkelers face to face with colorful creatures of the Caribbean.

DISNEY'S BLIZZARD BEACH®

Guests get all the spine-chilling thrills of a northern ski resort at Disney's Blizzard Beach water park, where Mt. Gushmore features moguls, slalom courses, toboggan and water sled runs, and the awesome, 120-foot-high Summit Plummet—the world's tallest, fastest free-fall speed slide. The sandy beach below Mt. Gushmore offers a large wave pool, a lazy stream, and children's play areas.

GOLF AROUND THE WORLD

Walt Disney World Resort is home to five 18-hole golf courses, making it one of the largest golf resorts in the country. These world-class courses host more than 400 tournaments each year. The newest courses are Disney's Osprey Ridge and Disney's Eagle Pine, joining Disney's Magnolia, Palm, and Lake Buena Vista courses as tournament venues. Guests also enjoy an additional golf area, Disney's Oak Trail, a family-play 9-hole walking course.

Miniature golf entertains and engages golfers of all ages on four whimsical courses. Fantasia Gardens Miniature Golf Courses, top and bottom left, are two 18-hole courses inspired by Disney's classic film *Fantasia*. Above and left, Disney's Winter Summerland is a wacky, elf-sized golf course with two 18-hole experiences. A study in bizarre contrasts, one course sports a zany, snow-clad Florida look, while the other takes a more tropical, holiday theme, with ornaments hanging from palm trees.

Disney's Wide World of Sports™ Complex

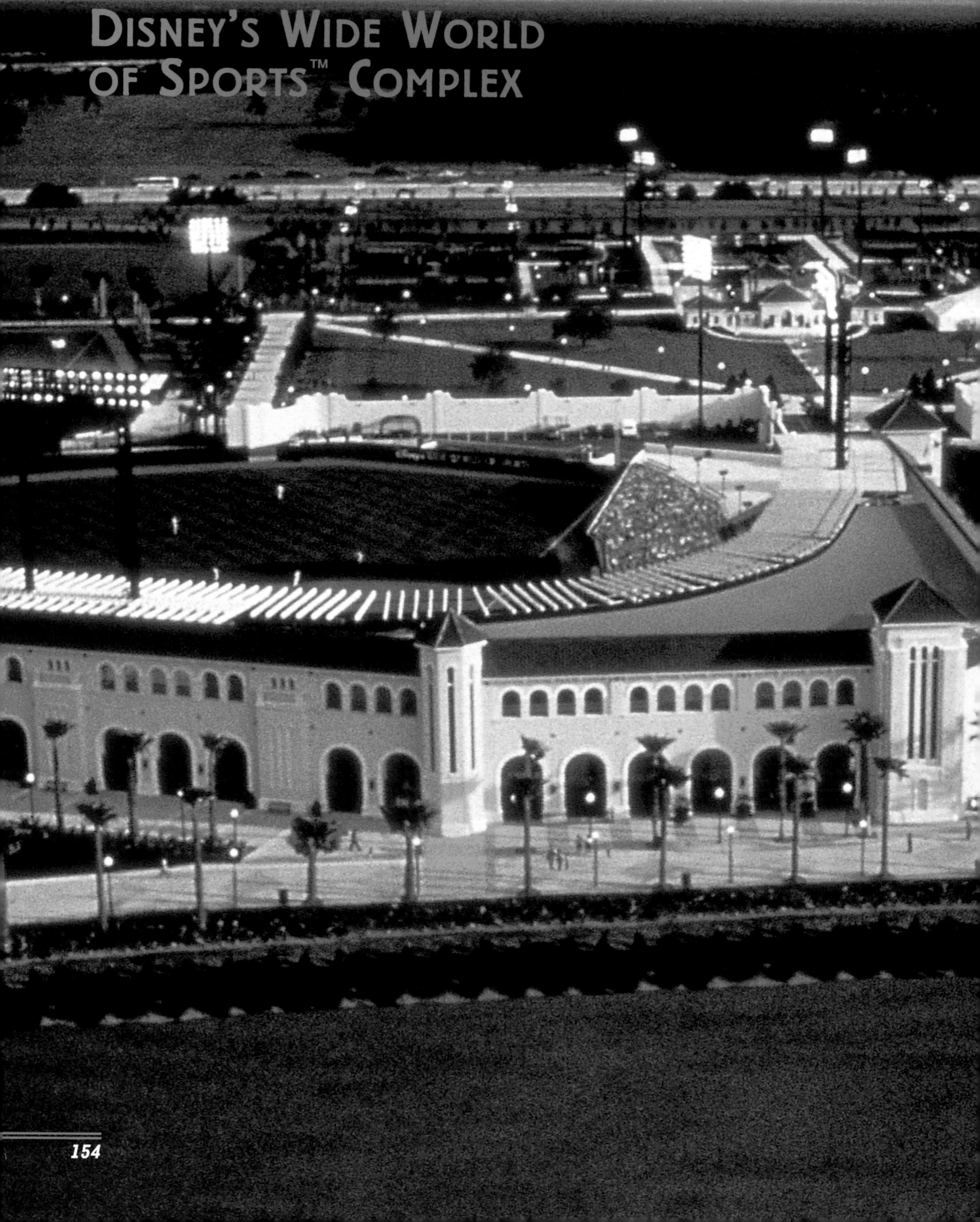

Thousands of athletes have traveled from around the world for a chance to make their mark at this state-of-the-art complex. The spectacular venues and perfectly manicured fields and diamonds host more than 30 sports, ranging from aerobics to wrestling.

DISNEY CRUISE LINE® SERVICES

Guests can enjoy three or four magical nights at the Walt Disney World Resort, then set sail to the Bahamas and Disney's own private island paradise, Castaway Cay, on the *Disney Magic* and *Disney Wonder* cruise ships, all part of the Seven-Night Disney Cruise Line Land and Sea Vacation. Designed specifically with areas and activities that appeal to every family member, this unique cruise experience offers original Disney musicals and first-run Disney films and animated classics, spas and sports, an adults-only entertainment district, and innovative rotation dining. The *Disney Magic* and *Disney Wonder* celebrate the legendary ocean liners of the 1930s, but with playful touches that are pure Disney.

CASTAWAY CAY

A one-of-a-kind adventure on Disney's private Bahamian island fills the final day of every Disney Cruise Line vacation. Strolling off the cruise ship and onto the dock, guests can enjoy miles of white-sand beaches, acres of pristine waters for swimming and water sports, and shady groves for bicycling on the 1,000-acre tropical paradise. And while youngsters are entertained at Scuttle's Cove, adults can head for Serenity Bay, a secluded beach on the island's north side that offers open-air massages in private cabanas overlooking the sea.

SEE YA LATER, MON!

DINING ON BOARD

A variety of unique dining experiences aboard the ships of the Disney Cruise Line make for many delicious days at sea. The adults-only restaurant Palo, right, features champagne brunches and a breathtaking 180-degree view of the ocean. Triton's, middle, on the *Disney Wonder*, offers under-the-seafood with casual elegance. Disney animation springs to life throughout your meal at the Animator's Palate, below right, and favorite Disney friends join families at colorful character breakfasts, below left.

T he Downtown Disney Area is an exciting, ever-growing metropolis, inspired by traditional downtowns from coast to coast. Stretched along the waterfront, it encompasses three distinct areas—Downtown Disney West Side, Downtown Disney Pleasure Island, and Downtown Disney Marketplace, where you can find exciting shopping, dining, and entertainment from morning until well after midnight.

Downtown Disney®

DOWNTOWN DISNEY WEST SIDE

The hip newcomer of the Downtown Disney area features some of the world's most exciting restaurants, nightclubs, and shopping adventures, offering an over-the-top experience that makes Downtown Disney one of Florida's premier entertainment destinations.

CIRQUE DU SOLEIL®

Artistic energy reaches new heights in the original production *La Nouba*™, at the Cirque du Soleil theater at Downtown Disney West Side. The *La Nouba* show transforms the ordinary into the extraordinary, replete with original music, surreal sets, extraordinary costumes, and high-energy choreography. Featuring high-wire and flying trapeze, stunning acro-gymnastic performances, and other dynamic displays of strength and coordination, the *La Nouba* show weaves an unforgettable tapestry of art, life, surprises, and high drama.

Photography by Veronique Vial. Costumes by Dominique Lemieux

DISNEYQUEST®

DisneyQuest Indoor Interactive Theme Park combines the magic of Disney with cutting-edge interactive technologies. The fun begins at the Ventureport, a crossroads which leads to five floors of one-of-a-kind rides, games, and attractions such as a swash-buckling shipboard adventure or a wacky bumper car ride.

DINING AT DOWNTOWN DISNEY® WEST SIDE

Created by Superstar Gloria Estefan and her husband Emilio, Bongos Cuban Cafe™, left, brings the sizzle of Miami's South Beach to Disney with authentic Cuban cuisine, Latin rhythms, and a tropical theme.

House of Blues®, top, is one of the hottest tickets in town, featuring mouth-watering Delta cuisine, live music in both the restaurant and concert hall, authentic folk art and a world-renowned, spirit uplifting Sunday Gospel Brunch. Planet Hollywood®, above, serves food from the stars! Literally. It's a fun dining experience inspired by the worlds of film and television, featuring tempting celebrity favorites in an out-of-this-world atmosphere of Hollywood memorabilia.

Celebrity chef Wolfgang Puck brings his award-winning cuisine and "Live, Love, Eat"® philosophy to Disney at the lively Wolfgang Puck® Cafe, where an exhibition kitchen adds a high-energy buzz. Guests line up for Puck's trademark pizzas and other delicious choices for lunch or dinner.

DOWNTOWN DISNEY® PLEASURE ISLAND

The fun is just beginning when the sun sets over the waters of *Downtown Disney* Pleasure Island. Every single night trendy party-goers jam the streets, nightclubs, boutiques, and restaurants of the 6-acre nighttime entertainment complex in a wild celebration of New Year's Eve—complete with fireworks, confetti, and laser strobes.

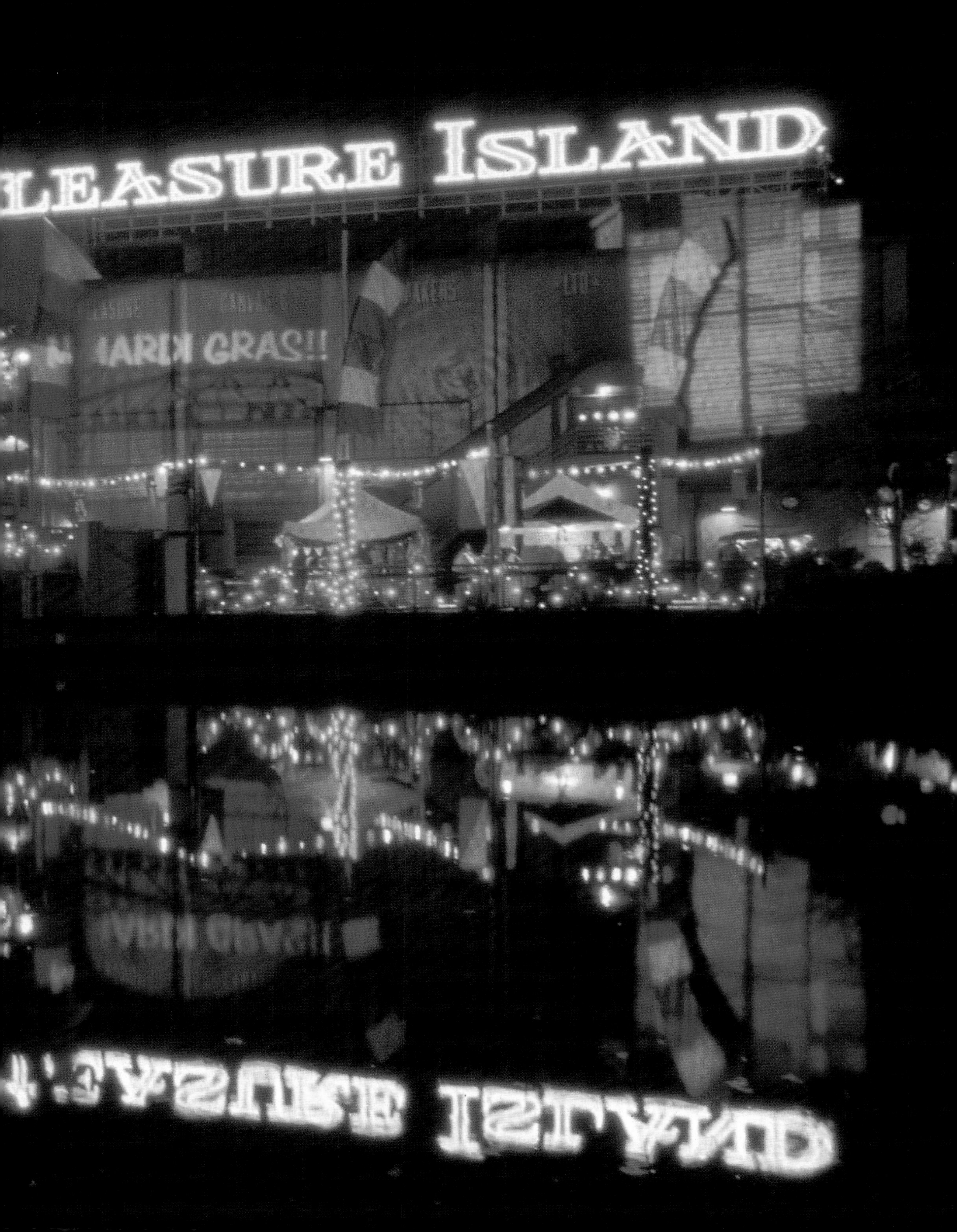
LEASURE ISLAND
MARDI GRAS!!

COMEDY WAREHOUSE

A live troupe of comedians, right, gives an uproarious improvisational show at the Comedy Warehouse, housed in a tiered theater where every seat offers a great view. Based on audience suggestions, the performance is truly improvised, so guests can return throughout the evening and never see the same show twice.

BET SoundStage™ Club

BET SoundStage Club keeps the energy high with a veejay who cues up videos by contemporary urban artists, chats with guests, and gets everyone on the dance floor. The club also features the best of rhythm and blues, soul, and hip-hop in live performances, and hosts programs aired on the BET Network.

ADVENTURERS CLUB

An eccentric cast of characters greets visitors to the Adventurers Club. The walls are loaded with trophy heads, photographs, and odd memorabilia, from the ridiculous to the sublime. Many of the intriguing objects were gathered in Africa, Asia, and the Pacific, while others were flea market finds—they create the perfect balance for this zany gathering spot. Each evening, the library opens and resident adventurers spin hilarious tales of their far-flung exploits.

8TRAX

Dance back in time to the gloriously gaudy days of lighted disco balls and dance floors where polyester reigned supreme. The mood of the 70s lives at 8Trax, as well as the sound. You're sure to catch dance fever when you slip on your platform shoes and do the hustle or boogie down at the house that funk built.

MANNEQUINS DANCE PALACE

The dance floor and light show set the standard for this award-winning club, designed with catwalks, stage rigging, and mannequins to give the illusion of a giant theatrical warehouse. The huge floor actually spins at different speeds, and speakers for the club's powerful sound system are built into the surface.

ROCK 'N ROLL BEACH CLUB

Nostalgic beach music is the theme, and live bands perform hits from the 1960s to the present. The surfer style décor permeates three stories of memorabilia, a large dance floor, billiard tables, and games.

WEST END STAGE

The famed West End Stage hosts top performers throughout the year. Every evening revelers gather to watch the electrifying moves of the Island Explosion Dancers, who perform the finale of the late-night New Year's Eve street party amid fireworks, special-effects lighting, and confetti.

PLEASURE ISLAND JAZZ COMPANY

The mood is contemporary 90s at the Pleasure Island Jazz Company, featuring recording artists and stars from around the world. Even guests sitting in the back of the house feel right on stage in this acoustically perfect performance room with a state-of-the-art sound system.

DOWNTOWN DISNEY® MARKETPLACE

Unique lakeside shops—everything from Disney animation art to
Disney apparel—delightful restaurants, expansive sidewalks, and
plenty of spaces for youngsters to stop and play add another
dimension to the Disney experience. Guests can even rent their
own boat or take a fishing excursion from Cap'n Jack's Marina.
And there are always special festivities at the Marketplace,
including holiday performances and one of the top judged art
shows in the Southeastern United States.

LEGO®
IMAGINATION
CENTER

Truly a kid's dream come true, the LEGO Imagination Center showcases the unlimited creative potential of LEGO® toys. Larger-than-life models built with millions of LEGO® elements are scattered outside the center, including an entire family with a snoring grandpa asleep on a bench. The center also features an outdoor, hands-on play area filled with hundreds of thousands of the plastic building blocks.

DINING AT DOWNTOWN DISNEY® MARKETPLACE

Dining options abound at Downtown Disney Marketplace, from Rainforest Cafe®, above, a wild place to shop and eat in a unique rain forest setting, to Fulton's Crab House, below, a three-deck dining emporium on a riverboat, which features seafood favorites flown in daily from ports around the world. Other dining spots include Ghirardelli® Soda Fountain & Chocolate Shop, offering wall-to-wall chocolates and ice-cream delights by San Francisco's notable sweet maker, and McDonald's®, serving its world-famous food in a Ronald's® Fun House–themed restaurant.

WORLD OF DISNEY

This superstore is the biggest
Disney character shopping adventure
in the world. Twelve areas each tell
their own story based on a classic
Disney film. To illustrate the theme
of travel throughout the store,
18 colorful murals depict famous
Disney characters venturing to
places around the globe.

From the moment they arrive, guests at Walt Disney World resorts enter a world of gracious hospitality and VIP treatment. Whether the choice is a luxury resort or a cabin in the wilderness, vacationers are immersed in the magic of Disney 24 hours a day.

RESORTS

DISNEY'S ANIMAL KINGDOM LODGE

Surrounded by 33 acres of re-created savanna land, the balconied rooms and four-story observation window of the newest Walt Disney World Resort hotel provide an incredible opportunity to view the more than 100 birds and animals that make this wildlife reserve home. Thatched roofs, rich and colorful artifacts, and vibrant artwork evoke African game lodges of years past, allowing guests to go on safari without leaving the comfort of their rooms.

DISNEY'S GRAND FLORIDIAN RESORT & SPA

Disney's picturesque "jewel in the crown" recalls the days when northerners made their annual winter pilgrimage to the fabled Florida beach resorts. The historic theme is completed by palms, southern magnolias, and richly colored gardens, which surround the hotel's 900 rooms, five restaurants, and luxurious spa and health club.

Dining Out

Victoria and Albert's

With just 65 seats, this intimate dining room is the crème de la crème of Disney dining. Guests receive personalized menus and impeccable service at tables set with fine china and silverware. For a special occasion, reserve the exclusive Chef's Table in the kitchen.

DISNEY'S CONTEMPORARY RESORT

Dining Out

California Grill

Extraordinary cuisine is served in this upscale hot spot on the top floor of Disney's Contemporary Resort. An incredible view of Magic Kingdom Park complements the equally incredible creations coming from the kitchen of Chef Clifford Pleau.

The first Walt Disney World Resort hotel is still one of the favorites, a creative A-frame design with great views of Magic Kingdom Park from many of its rooms and the sleek monorail gliding through its middle. Two delightful 90-foot high mosaic murals depicting children from around the world cover the walls in the lobby, right. The hotel offers 1,041 rooms and suites, three fine restaurants, and an expansive convention center.

DISNEY'S FORT WILDERNESS RESORT & CAMPGROUND

Guests who want room to stretch out and enjoy the great outdoors head for Disney's Fort Wilderness Resort & Campground, where cabins and campsites nestle in 740 acres of woodlands. There are hayrides, a petting farm, and fun-filled and relaxing activities from canoeing and bicycling to horseback riding. When night falls, guests can roast marshmallows and share stories while sitting around old-fashioned campfires.

THE VILLAS AT THE DISNEY INSTITUTE

The Villas at the Disney Institute are roomy and relaxing, perfect for families. Although only a short walk from the restaurants at Downtown Disney, each villa has a full kitchen, among other useful amenities. The octagonally-shaped Treehouse Villas stand on stilts and are surrounded by woodlands replete with chirping birds and crickets, beside scenic jogging and bicycling paths.

DISNEY'S WILDERNESS LODGE

The great lodges of the early national parks are the inspiration for Disney's Wilderness Lodge, which brings the rustic charm of the Rocky Mountains to Florida. A log-framed atrium with two 55-foot hand-carved totem poles and a massive stone fireplace captures the culture and beauty of the old park lodges, but with a contemporary flair. Outdoors, the hotel features a roaring waterfall and volcanic meadow with bubbling color pools, babbling brooks, and geysers spewing misty streams.

DISNEY'S CARIBBEAN BEACH RESORT

Sun-drenched colors and the characteristic architecture of five Caribbean islands—Martinique, Trinidad, Aruba, Barbados, and Jamaica—create this getaway. The 2,112-room resort stretches around Barefoot Bay, a pretty lake for boating bordered by a white-sand beach and a promenade that is perfect for walking or biking. Parrot Cay Island in the middle of the lake features a playground and paths for exploring.

DISNEY'S OLD KEY WEST RESORT

Inspired by America's southernmost city, Disney's Old Key West Resort is like a comfortable home away from home. It is distinguished by its spacious villas and community hall and plenty of activities for all ages. There is a lake for boating, a sprawling main pool with a fun children's area, and a casual restaurant serving delicious island specialties.

DISNEY'S PORT ORLEANS RESORT—FRENCH QUARTER

A wrought-iron entry gate leads to Port Orleans Square, where a village of ornate row houses re-creates the charm of the French Quarter, below. The scenic waterway connects the resort to nearby Disney's Port Orleans Resort—Riverside and Downtown Disney area. The colorful Doubloon Lagoon recreation area features comical Mardi Gras characters and a sea serpent water slide that emerges from the pool in a blaze of purple and turquoise.

DISNEY'S PORT ORLEANS RESORT—RIVERSIDE

Wandering paths, picturesque canals and the sounds of Cajun music paint a picture of Southern charm at Disney's Port Orleans Resort—Riverside. Guests can choose between mansion-style accommodations, left, and rustic retreats in the bayou. Many of the resort activities are at Ol' Man Island, a 3.5-acre recreation center with a swimming pool, playground, and fishing hole stocked with fish for catch and release.

DISNEY'S BOARDWALK INN AND VILLAS RESORT

Striped awnings and salt water taffy-colored facades recall the atmosphere of a turn-of-the-century boardwalk, when families and couples flocked to beach towns for innocent summertime fun. The colorful resort is designed to evoke a seaside village that grew and changed over the first decades of the 20th century, as if no single hand crafted it. The swimming pool, inset below, is inspired by the lighthearted Luna Parks that were built in a number of cities in the early 1900s.

Dining Out

The Flying Fish Cafe

Giant shimmering fish scales hug the columns, delicate lights dangle from oversized fish hooks, and sleek golden fish sculptures arc overhead at The Flying Fish Cafe, a trendy eatery that serves some of the finest seafood in America. The stage kitchen provides a high-energy dinner show, and a gold-tiled countertop offers casual dining right in front of the chefs.

DISNEY'S YACHT AND BEACH CLUB RESORTS

Across the lake from Disney's BoardWalk Inn Resort, these hotels feature two distinct looks: the sand-colored clapboard buildings of Disney's Yacht Club Resort and the pastel blue of Disney's Beach Club Resort. Both share a fabulous 3-acre water playground that features a life-sized shipwreck, left, and water slides. Bottom left, the lobby of Disney's Yacht Club Resort boasts millwork and brass with polished oak floors. The lighthouse, bottom right, welcomes home weary guests at the end of the day.

DISNEY'S POLYNESIAN RESORT

Disney's Polynesian Resort lies just minutes from the Magic Kingdom Park amid coconut palms and orchids, volcanic rock waterfalls, and white-sand beaches. Longhouses named for various Pacific Islands are scattered along the Seven Seas Lagoon. The nightly Polynesian Luau, below, features authentic Polynesian dancers and music, as well as a full Polynesian-style meal.

DISNEY'S CORONADO SPRINGS RESORT

Tile roofs, mosaic accents, and shades of sand, pink, and blue create a southwestern feel at Disney's Coronado Springs Resort, set on its own lagoon, Lago Dorado. The Dig Site area, right and bottom right, features a 50-foot-high Mayan pyramid with a water slide that spills into the pool, and a sandbox stocked with Mayan carvings waiting to be excavated. There are 1,967 rooms and suites in three Spanish-style villages—Casitas, Ranchos, and Cabanas, each with its own pool.

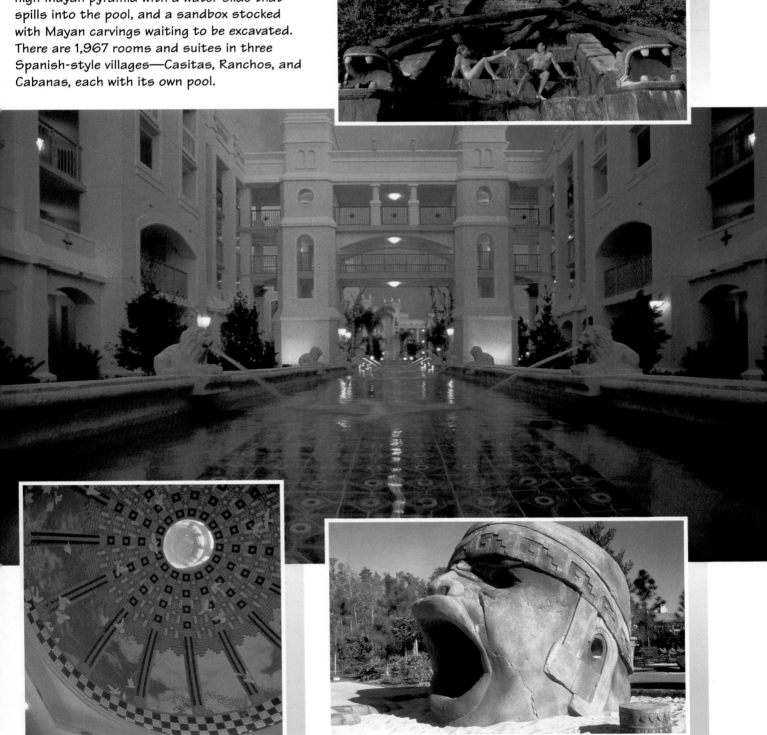

DISNEY'S ALL-STAR RESORTS

The most whimsical of all Walt Disney World Resort hotels, All-Star Resorts feature larger-than-life icons illustrating three diverse themes. Football helmets, surfboards, and stairwells in the shape of tennis ball cans draw sports fans to Disney's All-Star Sports Resort, right. Broadway, country, rock 'n' roll, and calypso themes are featured in Disney's All-Star Music Resort, below, and Disney's All-Star Movies Resort includes giant embellishments from favorite Disney films including *101 Dalmatians* and *Fantasia/2000*, opposite page.

DISNEY'S POP CENTURY RESORT

The newest lodging at the Walt Disney World Resort takes guests on a journey through American Pop Culture in the 20th Century, highlighting the toys, fads, technological breakthroughs, dance crazes, and catch phrases that defined each decade. Larger-than-life pop icons like bowling pins, a laptop computer, and cellular phones tower near the buildings.

Disney's Pop Century Resort scheduled to premiere March, 2002